LEGO HERO FACTORY

FACE OFF

MAKURO'S SECRET GUIDEBOOK

by Greg Farshtey

P9-CAA-270

ISBN 978-0-545-55235-6

LEGO and the LEGO logo are trademarks of the LEGO Group. © 2013 The LEGO Group. Produced by Scholastic Inc. under license from the LEGO Group.

Published by Scholastic Inc. SCHOLASTIC and associated logos are trademarks and/or registered trademarks of Scholastic Inc.

12 11 10 9 8 7 6 5 4 3 2 1   13 14 15 16 17/0

Printed in the U.S.A.   40
First printing, September 2013

TABLE OF CONTENTS

WELCOME TO
HERO FACTORY

Today, you begin your new life as a Hero. You have emerged from the Assembly Tower with the armor, equipment, and Hero Core you need to strike for justice in the galaxy.

Before you can begin your first mission, however, it is important that you understand the Heroes you will work alongside and the villains you will face. That is why you have been provided with this manual. Within these pages, you will meet the best and the worst robots this galaxy has to offer. You will also be privileged to view confidential computer projections of the outcome of battles between Heroes and villains, and even Heroes and Heroes.

WHAT IS HERO FACTORY?

Hero Factory is a private organization founded by Akiyama Makuro. It is located on a small planetoid near the Makuhero Asteroid Belt. Surrounded by the immense Makuhero City, Hero Factory is a symbol of the ideals of peace and justice for robots everywhere.

Mr. Makuro, the oldest-known robot, was a skilled inventor and a successful industrialist. He decided to put his vast fortune to good use and converted one of his robotics facilities into Hero Factory. Despite a rocky start, during which Mr. Makuro actually ordered the facility shut down and the team disbanded, Hero Factory went on to become a great success. It is now staffed by millions of worker robots who oversee the construction of new Heroes.

Hero Factory is recognized by virtually all planetary governments as a duly deputized law-enforcement agency. Although it is a private foundation, all Heroes work hand-in-hand with local law whenever possible. However, it is understood that Hero Factory exists to meet the challenges normal police agencies may not be able to handle on their own.

HOW ARE HEROES MADE?

Heroes begin their lives in the Furnace, where top-grade alloys are forged into the bodies of new robots. Once this is complete, the robots move up to the Assembly Tower, where nano-chips and servos are installed. Each and every Hero's design is different, as are the emotional capacitors and logic circuits that help make up their neural net. As a result, Heroes have different personalities and different sets of skills.

The key component of a Hero is the Hero Core, a power source containing a tiny sliver of the Quaza Stone. Each Hero Core is personally crafted by Mr. Makuro, who is the only one allowed access to the mysterious Quaza artifact. A Hero Core provides life-giving energy to its bearer and can be recharged as needed.

WARNING: Removal of your Hero Core can result in severe consequences, including the termination of your robotic existence. Do NOT allow opponents access to your Core.

THE HISTOTRON SECRET FILES

QUAZA

Quaza is an extremely rare mineral which is essential to the creation of Heroes and the operation of Hero Factory. While it is a great source of energy, it also has mutagenic properties and has been shown to transform creatures that have too much exposure to it.

Hero Factory features a Quaza Chamber, where Heroes can go to recharge their power Cores. Unauthorized use of the Quaza Chamber can result in permanent exile from Makuhero City, under Makuro Directive 5.7b-4.

MAKUHERO CITY

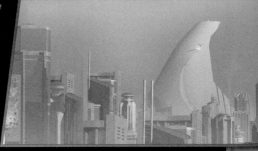

A sprawling metropolis, Makuhero City is home to the workers who keep Hero Factory running. As the location of Hero Factory, it has been targeted numerous times by villainous robots and alien species, but has so far survived intact.

In addition to housing Hero Factory, the city is also home to the prestigious Makuhero University. The university contains the only known working model of the Histotron, a device which allows the user to instantly access complete information on a range of past events.

RISE OF THE ROOKIES

PRESTON STORMER

HISTORY: One of the first Heroes created, Stormer served under Thresher in the first Alpha Team. After Thresher's retirement from active service, Stormer became the new leader of the team.

Stormer has completed more missions than any other active Hero. A master tactician, he continues to go on missions even when he should be back in Hero Factory overseeing operations. He is a stern leader and mandates constant training, especially of rookies.

PERSONALITY: Stormer has little sense of humor, works and trains harder than anyone, and can sometimes be short-tempered. He knows that if Hero Factory makes a mistake, civilians can be hurt, so he is determined never to make an error again.

EQUIPMENT: Ice armor; multi-functional ice weapon; removable Hero Core; command helmet with camera and communications headset

"NO MORE GAMES, ROOKIES. THINGS ARE ABOUT TO GET SERIOUS."

DUNKAN BULK

"I JUST TAPPED IT. HOW WAS I SUPPOSED TO KNOW THEY MAKE SPACESHIPS SO FRAGILE THESE DAYS?"

HISTORY: Bulk was part of the first Alpha Team and is one of the most respected veteran Heroes. He has a close relationship with Stormer.

New Heroes know they can rely on Bulk to help them train and learn the ins and outs of Hero Factory. Bulk remembers well how it felt to be a rookie and all the uncertainty of the early days of Alpha Team. He is always there to listen and offer support.

PERSONALITY: Bulk can be rough and tough, but he also has a great sense of humor and is quick to make jokes to relieve tension. Knowing he is the strongest Hero, he is quick to charge into a fight to protect the other Heroes.

EQUIPMENT: Metal sphere shooter; removable Hero Core; armor; helmet with camera and communications headset

JIMI STRINGER

HISTORY: Another member of the original Alpha Team, Stringer is a master of sonic weaponry and a skilled musician. Since he is used to studying the different layers of a song, he is always looking for the different layers in a situation as well. Stringer takes nothing at face value and is quick to ask questions, even of Stormer.

During the battle with Corroder on Tantalus, Stringer came up with the plan to use the power of Bulk's Hero Core to create an energy shield against the villain's weapon.

PERSONALITY: Stringer is always calm and cool. No matter the danger, he stays relaxed. His attitude is that he has had so many adventures and survived, there's nothing that can scare him now.

EQUIPMENT: Sonic boom weapon; removable Hero Core; armor; helmet with camera and communications headset

"HERE THEY COME, ROOKIES. LETS ROCK."

WILLIAM FURNO

"HEROES TO THE CORE!"

HISTORY: Furno was the first of a new breed of Hero manufactured at Hero Factory, and was eager to become a full-fledged part of Alpha Team. He resented it when Stormer kept him out of action.

But it was Furno's quick thinking that allowed him to bluff Corroder into thinking reinforcements were heading for Tantalus 5, prompting the villain to flee. All of this helped to cement his reputation as the most promising rookie in the history of Hero Factory.

PERSONALITY: Furno is headstrong, impatient, and overconfident, but he is also one of the most skilled Heroes ever created. Although he and Stormer had their share of clashes on early missions, Furno eventually came to realize that his conflicts with the Alpha Team leader came from his strong desire to prove himself to Stormer.

EQUIPMENT: Dual fire shooter; removable Hero Core; armor; communications helmet with camera

HERO
MARK SURGE

HISTORY: Surge is one of the more troubled active Heroes. Built using experimental methods, he repeatedly stated his fear that he would turn evil at some point. Despite this, he proved to be a capable Hero, if one who sometimes tries too hard.

Surge fought in the battles of Lemus 2, Mekron City, and New Stellac City. His most important contribution was the creation of a Hero Cell to protect the fallen Bulk and other Heroes from the power of Corroder.

PERSONALITY: Surge tries to cover his worries by throwing himself into dangerous missions. He can be defiant and emotional, especially if he feels his performance is being criticized. Stormer knows that, like a live wire, Surge has to be handled with care.

EQUIPMENT: Electrical shield; lightning weapon; removable Hero Core; armor; helmet with camera and communications headset

"I'LL TAKE THE MISSION. THE MORE DANGER, THE BETTER!"

NATALIE BREEZ

"WE'LL STOP YOU BECAUSE WE'RE HEROES... AND THAT'S WHAT HEROES DO."

HISTORY: Breez was the first Hero created under a new program designed to link the robots to the natural world. As a result, she is able to communicate with animals and can sense when something isn't right with a planetary environment.

In some of her early missions, Breez seemed to always be the one tending the wounded or evacuating civilian robots off-planet. But during the struggle with Von Nebula, she played a key role in curing Stormer of his nanobot-induced insanity and later helped defeat Corroder.

PERSONALITY: Breez is especially concerned about the safety of innocent victims who may get caught in the middle of battles with villains. Breez will go out of her way in a crisis to save civilians.

EQUIPMENT: Energized dual boomerang; removable Hero Core; armor; helmet with camera and communications headset

MELTDOWN

HISTORY: Every Hero's worst nightmare: a completely deranged and evil robot with a love for radioactive sludge. Unlike other villain robots who have simply gone wrong somewhere along the way, Meltdown was "built bad." Faulty logic circuits and a corrupted emotion chip combined to create a terrible menace to the galaxy. In his long career, Meltdown has done everything from theft and hijacking to the destruction of an entire city.

PERSONALITY: Meltdown is not a villain out of greed or even a desire for power . . . he's just mad and wicked to the Core. A minor genius when it comes to working with radioactive materials, he is considered by Hero Factory to be the most dangerous of all of Von Nebula's henchbots.

EQUIPMENT: Armor; radioactive sludge shooter; meteor blaster

"ANY HERO WHO CHALLENGES ME BETTER BE READY TO BURN."

CORRODER

"YOU HEROES ARE ALL SO TOUGH UNTIL YOU RUN INTO A LITTLE ACID."

HISTORY: Corroder's main career is sabotage for hire. Using his acid blaster, he caused untold damage around the galaxy and was one of the first villains recruited by Von Nebula for his gang.

PERSONALITY: Corroder once plotted to take over leadership from Von Nebula, but was willing to wait for the right moment to strike . . . which never came.

EQUIPMENT: Meteor blaster; acid blaster; armor

"EVERYBODY THINKS I'M DUMB ... UNTIL I GET MY HANDS ON THEM."

VILLAIN

THUNDER

HISTORY: Thunder was already wanted for extortion, theft, and the destruction of a trade fleet when Von Nebula hired him. He made a good follower, always willing to do what he was told.

PERSONALITY: Thunder is big and strong, but dumb, which every evil boss seems to prefer.

EQUIPMENT: Crusher claw; meteor blaster; nebula gas cannon; armor

XPLODE

"I DIDN'T ASK FOR MONEY, FURNO. I'M TAKING YOU DOWN FOR FREE."

HISTORY: Xplode was one of the more dangerous criminals because he was so successful that he didn't need the money and so smart he wouldn't walk into traps. He took on jobs just for the challenge.

PERSONALITY: He has no hesitation in betraying his partners for his own advantage.

EQUIPMENT: Explosive spikes; armor

ROTOR

HISTORY: After being accused of treason, Rotor migrated from his home world to continue his criminal career of robbery and assault.

PERSONALITY: Rotor is cruel and has an explosive temper. He considers Xplode to be his only friend, despite the fact that Xplode is always abandoning him in crisis situations.

EQUIPMENT: Rotor blade; meteor blaster; armor

"COME HERE AND LET ME CUT YOU DOWN TO SIZE!"

VAPOR

HISTORY: Little is known about Vapor. Von Nebula contracted Vapor to cause trouble as a distraction for Hero Factory, which led to imprisonment for his galactic crimes.

PERSONALITY: Unlike other villains, he has no real interest in vengeance on Hero Factory—he would prefer to just be left alone to rob and steal and destroy property.

EQUIPMENT: Vapor launchers; claws

"BREATHE DEEP, HERO . . . IT WILL BE THE LAST ONE YOU EVER TAKE."

VON NEBULA

HISTORY: Once, he was a Hero named Von Ness, a member of the first Alpha Team. From the start, he did not have the same commitment to his duty. During a battle with a giant robot in New Stellac City, Von Ness panicked and fled. When he returned, he had rebuilt himself into a villain called Von Nebula, with power over gravity through his Black Hole Orb Staff and a plot to destroy Hero Factory.

NOTE: In an alternate dimension visited by Alpha Team, he wound up ruling a criminal empire.

EQUIPMENT: Black Hole Orb Staff; armor

"TREMBLE, HEROES, BEFORE THE POWER OF GRAVITY UNLEASHED."

RISE OF THE ROOKIES

Stormer was uncertain about his new team. Although Alpha Team still had veterans like Stringer and Bulk, there were also three rookies on the team: Breez, Furno, and Surge. How would they hold up in battle? Memories of other Heroes who had cracked under pressure made Stormer drive the rookies hard to make sure they were ready for whatever came their way.

They got their first major test when reports came in of an attempt to steal explosives on Merak 9. Stormer's team fought two villains, Xplode and Rotor, and succeeded in capturing Rotor (though he later escaped). A second raid on an explosives plant on Lemus 2 by the two villains was also foiled.

Meanwhile, Corroder launched an attack on the construction site for a new prison on Tantalus 5. Hero Factory responded, but this time barely survived the encounter with the powerful villain. Stormer began to wonder if all these attacks might be related somehow.

Things took a more dangerous turn when the villain Meltdown infected Drax, the police chief of Mekron City, with nanobots that turned him evil. When Hero Factory showed up to investigate, Meltdown ambushed them and infected Stormer. After a prolonged chase and fight, Stormer was finally captured and cured.

The power behind all these attacks was finally revealed when the Heroes faced off with the villains in New Stellac City. A powerful villain, Von Nebula, announced that he was behind the plot to destroy Hero Factory. He had once been a Hero himself, named Von Ness, a member of Stormer's original team. He battled Stormer and Furno inside a black hole while his henchbots fought the other Heroes. After a fierce fight, Stormer succeeded in trapping Von Nebula inside his own Black Hole Orb Staff. The other villains were defeated and imprisoned as well.

DROPSHIP

Dropships are the primary means of Hero transport. Produced in a variety of sizes, dropships can carry anywhere from one to twelve Heroes. The rear compartment contains Hero pods, small circular craft that Heroes can ride in to reach the surface of a planet.

Each dropship is armed with an H-force launcher and a cockpit vario-field. More recent models are fitted with chameleon circuits, allowing the craft to be disguised either in flight or upon landing.

FURNO BIKE

The Furno Bike was a prototype developed in the Hero Factory labs prior to Alpha Team's battle with Von Nebula. Originally called the "Blaze Bike," it got its new name when Furno adopted the vehicle as his own.

The Furno Bike is equipped with dual plasma blasters and is powered by a nucleonic engine. Its tires are specially treated so they will not melt at high speeds. It can hold one rider, but it is recommended that robots receive extra training first to enable them to handle the vehicle.

ZIB

Nathaniel Zib is the Senior Mission Manager for Hero Factory. It's his job to make sure the Heroes have the information and equipment they need to get the job done. Zib is a skilled strategist and often consults with Stormer on the best line-up for a given mission.

"Everyone knows about us," Stormer said once. "They know me or Bulk or Furno, and we get all the credit for saving the day. Zib is the Hero they don't see, and without him, we couldn't do what we do."

ALLIES

MR. MAKURO

Founder of Hero Factory, Akiyama Makuro is the oldest-known robot still in existence. Details of his construction are shrouded in mystery, but during his lifetime he has amassed a great wealth and a reputation as an inventor and industrialist.

Believing that wealth should be used for the greater good, Mr. Makuro launched Hero Factory, the galaxy's first private law-enforcement body. It has now become an indispensable part of daily life, with Heroes known far and wide for their good deeds and life-saving feats.

THE HISTOTRON SECRET FILES

PLACES

LEMUS 2: A barren, rocky planet whose only important feature was an explosives plant. This was raided by Xplode and Rotor.

MEKRON CITY: A heavily populated urban center in the Mekronite Planetoid Belt, its local law enforcement was headed by Chief Drax. Meltdown ambushed the Heroes here after corrupting Drax.

MERAK 9: A mining asteroid attacked by Xplode and Rotor during their attempt to steal C-4000 explosive.

NEW STELLAC CITY: Site of Von Ness' original betrayal of Hero Factory and later the location of a showdown between Von Nebula and his gang and the Heroes. The main city park features a statue of Stormer.

TANTALUS 5: Future site of Penitentiary 1331. Corroder attacked the half-constructed building as a way to lure the Heroes into battle.

OBJECTS

ANTIGRAVITY THRUSTER RINGS: Devices built into the Heroes' boots to allow them to fly. Furno used these to destroy Von Nebula's black-hole vortex.

BLACK HOLE ORB STAFF: Weapon used by Von Nebula to create areas of intense gravity. The weapon was stored at Hero Factory and eventually used to spark a mass breakout from the prison.

PARTICLE SEPARATOR: A device that temporarily causes the molecules of its user to drift apart. This was used by the Heroes to successfully evade explosive spikes fired by Xplode.

HERO CELL: A force field created by tapping into the power of a Hero Core. Surge created a cell using power from the wounded Bulk's core to resist the attack of Corroder.

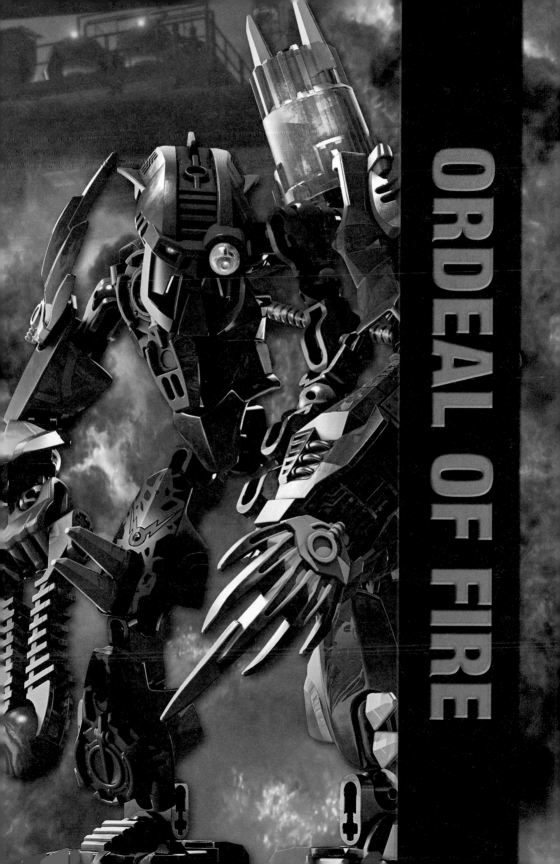

ORDEAL OF FIRE

STORMER 2.0

HISTORY: Whenever Stormer begins to feel overconfident in his abilities, he remembers the battle of Tanker Station 22. Initially believing the raid on the station was just another pirate attack, he took a team of all rookies to investigate. They rapidly found themselves outpowered and had to retreat to Hero Factory.

Once there, Stormer argued with Mr. Makuro to allow Alpha Team to experience Upgrade. Makuro suggested sending Evo and Nex after Fire Lord and his crew, but Stormer made it clear that the honor and reputation of Alpha Team was at stake.

EQUIPMENT: Multi-tool ice shield (includes ice blade and ice spike missiles); extendable baton

FURNO 2.0

HISTORY: Furno does not look back on this mission with great pride. After the fight with Von Nebula, Furno believed he had nothing left to learn about being a Hero. He was wrong—he still had to master the self-discipline to know when to follow orders and when to take initiative.

Following the defeat at Tanker Station 22 and the Upgrade, Furno found that he was having a hard time mastering his new weapon in Virtual Training. During the battle, his weapon became interlocked with Breez's, leaving them both vulnerable to attack. If not for the timely appearance of Nex, who freed them, it's possible both Heroes might have been badly injured. Following Fire Lord's capture, Furno spent a great deal of time reviewing tapes of this mission to try and learn from it.

EQUIPMENT: Multi-tool ice shield (includes cutting blades, rotating climbing hooks, and dual-fire blaster)

NEX 2.0

HISTORY: Nex was constructed using 2.0 technology. It was originally intended that he and Evo would be part of a new team of 2.0 Heroes, which would act as a strike force in situations where rapid response was required. While that idea never got off the ground, on this mission, that was exactly what he and Evo ended up being.

Sent to Tanker Station 22 to aid Alpha Team, Nex defeated Nitroblast. He then saved the lives of Breez and Furno, letting them both get back into the fight. It was easily the best performance by a rookie in battle since that of Furno. It even managed to impress Stormer.

EQUIPMENT: Multi-tool ice shield (includes ice blaster, pneumatic pincers, and circular cutting blades)

"LET ME TAKE A LOOK AT IT. THERE'S NO TECH I CAN'T FIGURE OUT."

EVO 2.0

"I CAN TAKE CARE OF MYSELF. JUST STAY OUT OF MY WAY!"

HISTORY: Evo was one of the first Heroes ever to be built using 2.0 technology. Mr. Makuro had hopes that this tech would enable him to transcend the usual rookie level and be part of the core of a new team. Although Evo would prove to be a brave and capable Hero, he did not end up rising to the level of Bulk or Stringer on his first adventure.

Evo, along with Nex, was dispatched by Zib to Tanker Station 22 to aid Stormer's team. They arrived in a Hero pod just in time to turn the tide of battle against Fire Lord and his gang. While Evo fought well, he was still assigned to the rookie team after.

EQUIPMENT: Multi-tool ice shield (includes double-barreled ice cannon)

HERO
SURGE 2.0

HISTORY: When Surge, Stormer, and the other Heroes were being overpowered by Fire Lord and his gang, Surge caused a distraction to allow his teammates to escape. Although he was believed lost in the explosion, he survived and was captured by the criminals. They planned on holding him for ransom, but he managed to later escape and set up the criminal mastermind's defeat.

After the battle, Surge received a commendation for bravery and an Upgrade to 2.0.

EQUIPMENT: Ice-spear blaster

HERO
BREEZ 2.0

HISTORY: When Breez first arrived on Tanker Station 22, she knew immediately what her priority had to be: saving the civilian workers of the refueling plant from the fury of Fire Lord.

When the Heroes returned to Hero Factory, Breez had the honor of presenting Surge with his ice-spear launcher after he was Upgraded to 2.0. Since they were such good friends, it meant a great deal to both of them to share that special day.

EQUIPMENT: Multi-tool blades

FIRE LORD

"EVERY MOMENT YOU HEROES EXIST FROM NOW ON, YOU DO SO ONLY THROUGH MY MERCY."

HISTORY: Fire Lord is a perfect example of a good idea gone bad. Once a basic mining robot, he was Upgraded to be able to absorb fuel directly through his hands. The tremendous heat and energy caused some of his wiring to fuse, driving him mad and making him want to conquer the galaxy.

PERSONALITY: Fire Lord has a tremendous ego and a great deal of raw power. Although not at the level of a Von Nebula or a Black Phantom in terms of being a master criminal, his sheer insanity and total lack of regard for innocent robots who might get in his way put him on Hero Factory's "Most Wanted" list.

EQUIPMENT: Lava-sphere shooter; lava flamethrower

NITROBLAST

"IF YOU CAN'T STAND THE HEAT, STAY AWAY FROM ME."

HISTORY: Nitroblast was a malfunctioning mining robot who went to work for Fire Lord. In his brief criminal career, he racked up charges of arson, assault, extortion, and theft of government property. Nitroblast was part of the gang during the assault on Tanker Station 22, and helped defeat Alpha Team in that battle.

PERSONALITY: Although powerful and destructive, Nitroblast is actually as much of a planner as a doer. His earliest crimes involved safecracking, and he was known among the other gang members for being patient and methodical. He blames Hero Factory for the "death" of Fire Lord and has vowed vengeance.

EQUIPMENT: Plasma torch; lava-sphere shooter

JETBUG

HISTORY: Jetbug was a pilot for a mining operation until he decided there was more profit to be made in crime. After that, he started a career of robbery, assault and arson.

PERSONALITY: Some records indicate that Jetbug has spent so much time in the air that he loses his sense of balance when he is on the ground.

EQUIPMENT: Lava-sphere shooter; razor-sharp pincers

"I DON'T CARE HOW FAST YOU ARE, HERO. NEXT TO ME, YOU'RE STANDING STILL."

DRILLDOZER

HISTORY: Drilldozer was one of the more powerful mining robots to join up with Fire Lord. Although not the brightest member of the gang, Drilldozer was smart enough to know that having partners would give him an edge.

PERSONALITY: Drilldozer doesn't try to make complicated plans. He smashes, grabs what he wants, and leaves—and he doesn't say much while he's doing it.

EQUIPMENT: Lava-sphere shooter; multi-tooth turbine-powered drill; molten spikes; claws

"TIME TO PLAY 'BOUNCE THE HERO.'"

ORDEAL OF FIRE

Zib presented Alpha Team with dire news: A new team of villains was attacking Tanker Station 22, an important fuel depot. Stormer led Breez, Furno, and Surge to the site, only to have the team be soundly defeated by Fire Lord and his henchbots Drilldozer, Jetbug, and Nitroblast.

Returning to Hero Factory, the team met new Heroes Evo and Nex, both of whom had been created using the new 2.0 technology. Alpha Team (except for Surge, who was captured by villains) received the Upgrade as well, gaining fire-resistant armor.

They returned to the station, now in enemy hands, and confronted the villains in a final battle. With Surge's help, Stormer was able to capture Fire Lord, while the other Heroes stopped his gang cold.

UPGRADE

Despite the long years of Alpha Team's service, this was the first time they had ever been through the Upgrade process. Although Mr. Makuro had developed the basic concept some time back, he had hesitated to expose any existing Heroes to it for fear that the process might do damage.

Makuro deemed it safer to create new Heroes with the 2.0 armor and weapons, and so had Evo and Nex made. Although fire resistant, these two lacked Stormer's experience in battle. Despite the risk, Makuro eventually agreed to let Alpha Team go through Upgrade.

After undergoing the process, Stormer and the three rookies were put through Virtual Training to learn how to use their new bodies. Normally, this training takes six to eight weeks, but Stormer cut it short after less than a day. This was, he decided, an emergency situation and there was no further time for practice.

Fortunately, even with the reduced training time, the 2.0 armor and weapons performed flawlessly and the mission was a success. Since then, Upgrade has become a frequently used process whenever Hero Factory encounters a situation that requires specialized equipment.

PLACES

TANKER STATION 22: This facility is used for refueling of Hero vehicles and equipment. It consists of a circular building surrounded by and containing fuel cells. It is one of a number of such stations scattered around the galaxy. Although it is intended for use by Hero Factory personnel, Mr. Makuro often allows local governments or law enforcement to make use of the facilities.

Fire Lord's attack on the station was prompted by his desire for the fuel cells, which he was able to directly absorb in order to power himself. It was the lure of these cells that kept him and his gang from leaving the station after their initial victory over Hero Factory. Had they fled, it might have taken much longer for Alpha Team to track them down and stop them.

SAVAGE PLANET

ROCKA 3.0 / ROCKA XL

HISTORY: Returning from a successful mission, Rocka received a distress call from the planet Quatros. When he arrived there, he was ambushed and badly defeated by the Witch Doctor. His disappearance prompted Alpha Team to come to the planet to investigate.

Rocka was given an Upgrade while on the planet, receiving the raw strength of a lion. In the end, Furno and Rocka worked together to stop the crisis. Donning ancient armor found in a cave, Rocka became the bigger and more powerful Rocka XL. He helped to fight off the Witch Doctor until Stormer finally found a way to defeat the villain. Stormer recognized him for his bravery, but what no one knew at the time was that Rocka was not just any rookie. . . .

EQUIPMENT: Crossbow; energy shield

NEX 3.0

HISTORY: When Nex found out that his friend Rocka was in trouble on Quatros, he insisted on going along on the rescue mission. He received an Upgrade to 3.0 armor, gaining the power of a saber-toothed tiger.

Nex assisted Furno in trying to find a way to restore the Quaza that the Witch Doctor had stolen to the planet. In the end, it would be Bulk who would help to solve the problem. While he was doing that, Nex discovered a cache of Quaza spikes guarded by a mutant serpent. Nex defeated the creature and destroyed the spikes.

Following this adventure, Nex was dispatched to the frontier for a brief time to investigate rumors of dangerous scientific experiments (he found no evidence). He was back at Hero Factory when the mass breakout occurred.

EQUIPMENT: Double-bladed tiger claw

BULK 3.0

HISTORY: Bulk never liked the idea of Rocka being sent alone to Quatros to investigate the mysterious distress signal. "Sending a rookie in by himself will just make it worse," he said. Events proved him right, as the disappearance of Rocka forced Alpha Team to launch a search. Bulk was Upgraded to wolf armor, which enhanced his speed.

On the planet, Bulk teamed with Rocka and Stormer to use a teleportation bridge in an effort to catch up to Witch Doctor. The bridge malfunctioned and all three Heroes were shrunk down to only a couple of inches in height. Bulk and Rocka were captured by the Witch Doctor, but escaped with the help of Furno, Nex, and Stringer.

EQUIPMENT: Wrist-mounted blades

HISTORY: Stormer found that this mission was yet another in which he felt responsible for the crisis. He had been the one who had caught Hero Factory instructor Aldous Witch while trying to steal a Hero Core for personal use, an act that got Witch exiled. Now, as the Witch Doctor, the ex-instructor was threatening an entire planet and potentially the galaxy. Stormer was Upgraded to new 3.0 armor, which gave him the increased strength of a rhinoceros.

On their first adventure together, Rocka and Furno could not get along. It may be that Furno saw a little too much of himself in the headstrong rookie. Stormer reacted by splitting the team up, with one squad led by Rocka and one by Furno. This proved to be a wise decision, both because the mission was successful and because Rocka and Furno eventually ended up working well together.

EQUIPMENT: Dual-bladed sword capable of firing energy blasts

FURNO 3.0

HISTORY: Furno realized one thing right away when he arrived on Quatros: He really didn't like Rocka. First, the rookie disappears on a quarantined planet. Then Alpha Team has to go and rescue him, with Furno being Upgraded to hawk armor that allowed him to fly. And when they arrive, it seemed that he and Rocka could not agree on anything. Eventually, Stormer put Furno and Rocka in charge of separate units to remind them of the importance of teamwork.

Furno ended up helping Rocka craft the XL armor he used to fight Witch Doctor, as well as working with Bulk to restore the stolen Quaza to the planet. After the mission was over, Stormer praised him for managing to put aside his differences with Rocka for the good of the team. That, more than even his accomplishments in the field, meant Furno was no longer a rookie.

EQUIPMENT: Plasma bow

STRINGER 3.0

HISTORY: Seen from above, it was obvious that the continents had shifted on the planet Quatros. Stringer immediately guessed that someone was mining Quaza on the planet, for Quatros had been known to react in extreme fashion to any disturbance on its surface.

Armed with 3.0 armor that gave him the strength and endurance of a bear, Stringer joined his teammates on the search for Rocka. Discovering that the local wildlife had been mutated by Quaza energy and were now being controlled by Witch Doctor, Stringer led the fight to liberate the creatures.

Stringer has since made Quatros his personal cause. He consistently volunteers for the patrol of the sector to make sure the force field is intact and no miners or poachers have invaded the planet. Stormer encourages this, believing Heroes do best on missions they personally care about.

EQUIPMENT: Triple-bladed bear claw with built-in plasma gun

WITCH DOCTOR

HISTORY: Aldous Witch was an instructor at Hero Factory who envied the power of the Hero Cores which Stormer and the rest possessed. His attempt to supercharge himself with Quaza energy led to his dismissal from Hero Factory.

Witch traveled to the planet Quatros and began mining for Quaza. Exposure to Quaza energy and a strange skull he found on the planet transformed him into the Witch Doctor. He used Quaza spikes to take control of the native wildlife.

Alpha Team confronted him on Quatros after he lured them there with the intention of stealing their dropship. He was defeated through the combined efforts of Stormer and Rocka and imprisoned. He later escaped during the mass breakout from Hero Factory, but has since been recaptured.

EQUIPMENT: Skull staff; clawed launcher; Quaza spikes

"INSANE? IS IT INSANE TO SEE POWER AND WANT IT FOR YOURSELF?"

SCORPIO

HISTORY: Scorpio are rare, scorpionlike creatures who are intelligent and capable of speech. At least one was enslaved by the Witch Doctor and forced to attack members of Hero Factory, although it did so against its will. The beast was so powerful that even three Heroes working together could not stop it.

NATURAL TOOLS: Heavy armor plating; power pincers; Quaza stinger

"IT WOULD TAKE AN ARMY TO STOP ME— AND YOU DON'T HAVE AN ARMY."

RAWJAW

HISTORY: Rawjaws are apelike creatures native to the planet Quatros. They are extremely strong, highly agile, and the tusks beneath their lower jaw can penetrate any known armor. In the wild, they are very territorial and can be aggressive to intruders, but in general were never regarded as highly dangerous until Aldous Witch fitted some of the Rawjaws with Quaza spikes, which drove them into a frenzy.

NATURAL TOOLS: Armor plating; tusks

"FASTER, FASTER WE MUST WORK ... MORE QUAZA."

WASPIX

HISTORY: Waspix are insectoid creatures native to the protected planet Quatros. They spend most of their time in the air, and are rarely aggressive unless provoked. Witch Doctor managed to capture several Waspix and implant Quaza spikes in them, making the creatures much more dangerous. The Waspix are now back to living in peace on Quatros.

NATURAL TOOLS: Wings; toxic stingers

"GET OFF OUR PLANET, HEROES— YOU'RE NOT WELCOME HERE!"

FANGZ

HISTORY: Fangz are large hounds from the planet Quatros. They hunt in packs and are known for their ability to bring down animals much larger than themselves. The Witch Doctor used Quaza spikes to control several Fangz and used them as bodyguards. When the beasts were finally free of the villain's control, they actually showed affection to Rocka in gratitude for his help.

NATURAL TOOLS: Jaw spears

"GRRRRRRRR!"*

*FANGZ DON'T TALK. THEY JUST GROWL!

SAVAGE PLANET

The planet Quatros: Long quarantined for the safety of its ecosystem, it is one of the few remaining natural sources of Quaza. So when a distress call was heard coming from a planet where no one should have been, it was a mystery that had to be solved.

The nearest Hero to the planet was Rocka, but once he headed into the thick jungle of this wild planet, he was never heard from again. Alpha Team immediately headed out to find out what was wrong. Once there, they discovered that the force field that should have surrounded the planet was gone.

On the surface, the team encountered dangerous beasts with Quaza spikes implanted in them. These creatures were under the control of the Witch Doctor, an ex-employee of Hero Factory who lusted after the power of Quaza.

After a terrible struggle, the Heroes managed to overcome the Witch Doctor and free the enslaved beasts. The force field was restored and Quatros returned to being a peaceful world once more. Hero Factory has increased patrols in the area to prevent this sort of crisis from ever happening again.

PLACES

QUATROS

Quatros is a jungle planet that was once heavily mined by Hero Factory for Quaza. After a number of years, it was discovered that the mining was doing serious damage to the planet. Quatros was designated a protected planet and a wilderness preserve, and a force field was put in place around it.

The planet was once home to an ancient civilization, but little remains of them but artifacts and ruins. The creatures that are native to this world are techno-organic and seem to react to any change in the environment. Quatros itself is believed to be unusually sensitive to any external stimuli, and mining on its surface actually causes the shape of the continents to change.

Quatros has a tropical climate. There are currently no robots on the planet, only wild creatures in their natural environment. Some Hero Factory mining technology is also on the planet, but all of it is without power at this point. Mr. Makuro has vowed that Quatros will remain a protected world for as long as Hero Factory exists.

BREAKOUT

EVO

HISTORY: After the breakout, Evo was sent to Z'chaya to stop Toxic Reapa. Once he got there, he discovered cocoons holding the larvae of Toxic Reapa's species. His first plan was to try to destroy the cocoons, but Furno talked him out of it by radio, warning that efforts to do that might free the larvae instead.

Evo and Toxic Reapa battled, with the villain initially having the upper hand, but Evo finally outsmarted him and succeeded in slapping the Hero cuffs on. He then brought Toxic Reapa back to Hero Factory to imprison him again.

Once there, he found Rocka in a fight with Black Phantom. In the end, it was Evo's strategy that helped Rocka defeat the villain and end the crisis . . . for now.

EQUIPMENT: Tank arm; plasma gun; Hero cuffs

HISTORY: Rocka and Furno had returned from a successful mission to capture the electrical villain, Voltix. They didn't know that Voltix had planned to be captured so he could trigger a mass escape from the Hero Factory containment facility. Rocka was unable to stop him as he set the other prisoners free.

When the other Heroes went after the escaped villains, Rocka mysteriously remained behind. It was he who discovered that Black Phantom had arranged the breakout so that he could gain access to Hero Factory. Rocka battled the villain and his Arachnix drones, and with the help of Evo, succeeded in defeating him.

Rocka's revelation that he was a secret member of the Hero Recon Team came as a shock to the other Heroes.

EQUIPMENT: Crossbow; hex energy shield; helmet outfitted with infrared vision scope; Hero cuffs

STRINGER

HISTORY: Following the breakout, Stringer proceeded to the Tansari power collection array, which Voltix was in the process of converting into a weapon. Stringer attempted to get his Hero cuffs on the villain, but failed, and it began to look like this might be his last battle.

The struggle continued in the thick mist of Tansari VI. The battle seesawed back and forth, with Voltix gaining the advantage and then Stringer. In the midst of the fight, Stringer's hand stumbled upon his lost Hero cuffs and he was able to clap them on Voltix's wrists. The unique technology deadened Voltix's power and made it possible for Stringer to capture him.

By the time the two made it back to Hero Factory, the battle there was over. Stringer returned Voltix to prison and began working on increased security measures for the facility so such an event could not happen again.

EQUIPMENT: Sonic blaster; Hero cuffs

SURGE

HISTORY: The mission classified "Breakout" did not begin well for Surge. He was unable to prevent any villains from escaping and accidentally wound up manacled by a pair of Hero cuffs. However, after the battles with Fire Lord, Stormer had enough confidence in Surge to have him Upgraded with laser-proof armor and send him after Splitface on his own.

Surge discovered the villain attacking an important communications satellite in the Sigma Sigma system. The satellite was protected by a force field, but Splitface planned to shatter the field by targeting it with a large asteroid.

Confronting the villain in the asteroid field, Surge managed to avoid Splitface's blasts long enough to close in on him. After stunning the villain with electricity, Surge hurled him at the asteroid, shattering it before it could strike the force field. He then Hero-cuffed Splitface and returned him to jail.

EQUIPMENT: Electricity shooter; plasma gun; Hero cuffs

HISTORY: The evil industrial robot XT4 had a daring plan—he would return to the Makuro plant where he was first manufactured and where XT4 robots were still produced. There he would do a mass conversion of the robots to be villains like him, and lead a mechanical army against the occupied worlds.

By the time Nex arrived on the scene, XT4 had already begun his work. Nex had to fight through a legion of robots with altered programming to try to reach the true author of the villainy. When he finally reached XT4, his laser cutter had burned out.

Nex realized he had to use his wits if he was going to win. So when XT4 lashed out at him, he went down pretending he was knocked out. When XT4 turned back to his work, Nex surprised him from behind and subdued him with two pairs of Hero cuffs.

EQUIPMENT: Laser cutter; plasma gun; Hero cuffs

HISTORY: Bulk's mission was to apprehend Core Hunter. They had clashed in the past, and Core Hunter always pointed out that he thought Bulk was stupid. Bulk looked forward to proving him wrong.

After alerting the criminal underworld that he was looking for Core Hunter, Bulk took a dropship to one of the worlds Core Hunter had used as a hideout before, and made a big display of turning an old factory into a base of operations, knowing this would draw his old enemy out.

That night, Core Hunter broke in, spotted Bulk, and prepared to steal his Hero Core. What he didn't know was that "Bulk" was a spare robot from Hero Factory and only the Core was active. When he attacked the decoy, the real Bulk slammed him from behind and put on the Hero cuffs.

EQUIPMENT: Missile launcher; plasma gun; Hero cuffs

HERO
FURNO

HISTORY:
Furno's mission at first seemed quite strange: A Hero associated with fire was being sent underwater after Jawblade. But, being Furno, he was certain he would make short work of a villain who was never considered a master criminal.

He tracked Jawblade down and tried to apply the Hero cuffs, only to discover that they did not work underwater. But Jawblade had something that did: oxidium, which caused Furno's armor to stiffen and sent the Hero to the ocean floor. Fortunately, Furno was able to use the energies of his Hero Core to cancel out the power of the oxidium.

Capturing Jawblade, he returned him to prison. Once back at Hero Factory, he joined in the fight against Black Phantom's Arachnix drones while Rocka challenged the villain himself.

EQUIPMENT: Plasma gun with attached harpoon, designed for underwater use; Hero cuffs

BREEZ

HISTORY: When Stormer sent Breez to capture Thornraxx, she knew he must be going to Hive World, his home planet. Taking the fastest ship available, Breez managed to reach Hive World before her quarry, but not by much.

Thornraxx was enraged to find a Hero so close to his home—like the beast he resembled, he was very territorial and felt that Breez was "corrupting the nest." The battle that followed was among the wildest and most intense of any that followed the breakout, with Breez fighting for her life against the maddened villain.

In the end, Breez was able to use Thornraxx's rage against him. As he flew at her, she dodged, spun in space, and snapped the Hero cuffs on him as he flew by.

EQUIPMENT: Hex energy shield; plasma gun; twin-bladed sabre; Hero cuffs

HERO
STORMER XL

HISTORY: After the breakout, Stormer went after Speeda Demon. Outfitted with new armor and a high-speed cycle, he traveled to the ice planet Kollix IV to chase down the ultrafast villain.

Both Stormer and Speeda Demon's bikes moved so fast that they melted the ice underneath the tires, but then it refroze again almost instantly. In the end, it was Speeda Demon who miscalculated a turn and spun out of control. Stormer rescued him from what would have been a fatal plunge off a cliff and put the Hero cuffs on.

Since the close of this mission, Stormer has been working day and night, trying to trace to whom Black Phantom sent the Hero Factory plans . . . so far, without success. He is in constant contact with Mr. Makuro as they try to deal with this potentially massive threat to the safety of the galaxy.

EQUIPMENT: Power sword; plasma gun; Hero cuffs

CORE HUNTER

"I DIDN'T THINK THEY WOULD SEND YOU FOR THIS ONE, BULK. I THOUGHT THEY WOULD SEND ONE OF THE HEROES WITH A BRAIN."

HISTORY: Core Hunter is an ex-Hero who has become a thief and bounty hunter. He is known for attacking Heroes and stealing their Hero Cores, making him extremely dangerous.

Core Hunter escaped in the breakout but was recaptured by Bulk. He has numerous hideouts throughout the frontier region of space and has been known to use robot duplicates of himself to take his place in dangerous situations.

PERSONALITY: Methodical, devious, and cunning, Core Hunter prides himself on being able to anticipate what Heroes will do and set traps for them. Collecting Hero Cores has become an obsession for him, and he has actually gone out of his way to attack Heroes rather than escaping when he had the opportunity.

EQUIPMENT: Core-removal tool; multi-vision mask

XT4

HISTORY: XT4 began his life as one of many industrial robots manufactured by one of Mr. Makuro's plants. He was reprogrammed by the Legion of Darkness into being a villain. He later posed as a new Hero to try to infiltrate Hero Factory. He was captured along with the rest of the Legion and imprisoned, but escaped. Nex eventually tracked him down and re-arrested him.

PERSONALITY: XT4 has no emotions or social skills, as they were not a part of his original or his altered programming. He is incapable of any compassion or mercy.

EQUIPMENT: Razor disc slicer; laser slicer; two striking blades

"THE HEROES ARRIVED 3.67 MINUTES EARLIER THAN ESTIMATED, INDICATING MY CALCULATIONS OF THE STUN BEAM'S EFFECTIVENESS WERE OFF BY .001."

SPLITFACE

"LET'S TAKE THIS PLACE APART!"

HISTORY: Splitface was twice as dangerous as most villains, because he had two personalities. Half of his body was mechanical, and half was mutated organic matter, each with its own distinct identity. Splitface was a powerful enforcer, often forcing businessbots to pay him for "protection"—if they didn't pay, he destroyed their business.

Splitface was part of the original Legion of Darkness, but was captured by Stormer. He escaped during the mass breakout and attacked a communications satellite in the Sigma Sigma system. He was apprehended by Surge and thrown back in jail.

PERSONALITY: One of Splitface's identities is very rough and crude, while the other is colder and crueler. They are so different that they even prefer to use different weapons in battle. Splitface's reaction time in a fight can sometimes be slowed down when he starts arguing with himself.

EQUIPMENT: Shredding claw; poison plasma blaster

TOXIC REAPA

HISTORY:
Toxic Reapa, an insectoid native of the planet Z'chaya, was already an active criminal when Hero Factory came into being. Arrested after an attempted robbery by the new Heroes, he was broken out of prison by XT4 and joined the Legion of Darkness.

After yet another escape, he returned to Z'chaya with plans to create an insect army. His plot was stopped by Evo and he was imprisoned again. Security has been doubled around his cell after rumors that he may be planning another breakout, with help from other members of his species.

"IT'S FUN TO WATCH THE BIG, BRAVE HEROES SHAKING IN THEIR BOOTS."

PERSONALITY: Although extremely alien, Toxic Reapa has picked up the language, habits and attitudes of other criminals. He can be even more ruthless than some, at times doing things that shock even longtime crooks.

EQUIPMENT: Toxic jets; laser cutters

"YOU'RE IN MY ELEMENT NOW, HERO— AND NOBODY BEATS JAWBLADE IN THE WATER!"

HISTORY: Jawblade is a native of the water planet Scylla, and specialized in aquatic crimes. Early in his career, he attempted to rob a museum by entering via the feeder pipes that supplied water to the aquariums, but he was stopped by the newly active Hero Factory. He later joined the original Legion of Darkness and was part of the failed attempt to seize the Hero Factory facility.

After the breakout, the underwater villain returned to his home world, intending to seize vast stores of oxidium, which could be used to immobilize robots. He was pursued by Furno and the two fought underwater until the Hero finally succeeded in subduing him.

PERSONALITY: Jawblade is ruthless and easy to anger. Though he can function on land, he hates how awkward he looks when he walks on his fins.

EQUIPMENT: Twin magma blades

BLACK PHANTOM

HISTORY: Black Phantom has a long and dark history with Hero Factory. When Alpha Team was new, Black Phantom organized the Legion of Darkness, a gang of criminals dedicated to destroying Hero Factory.

Years later, Black Phantom was the guiding force behind the massive prison break that freed all the convicts held at Hero Factory. He used the chaos as a distraction so he could infiltrate and send the plans for Hero Factory to an unknown ally. He was defeated by Rocka and imprisoned, but refuses to reveal for whom he was working.

PERSONALITY: Black Phantom is extremely intelligent and very skilled at manipulating other villains. He is always looking for an angle that will benefit him.

EQUIPMENT: Razor Sabre Mace Staff; sabre strikers; Arachnix drone

"I WANT HERO FACTORY IN RUINS."

VILLAIN

SPEEDA DEMON

HISTORY: Speeda Demon is a master of the quick robbery and the even faster getaway. His rocket bike is faster than almost anything Hero Factory has, and he knows that as long as he keeps moving, he can stay free. He learned more than he wanted to about being in prison after his time with the Legion of Darkness, and will do anything he has to do to stay out of jail . . . except stop committing crimes.

PERSONALITY: Speeda Demon used to be a very rational, practical villain, with little time for the drama some other bad robots bring with them. Something happened during his time in prison, and he now seems to be quite insane, which only makes him more dangerous.

EQUIPMENT: Nitro rocket motorbike; wing blades

THORNRAXX

"HATE HERO FACTORY. HUNT THEM DOWN. MAKE THEM PAY."

HISTORY: Perhaps the most alien of all the villains Hero Factory has faced, Thornraxx is an insectoid being from a hive world. How he got to more populated planets and why he chose a life of crime remains a mystery.

PERSONALITY: Thornraxx does not understand how most robots behave. He is primitive and savage and gives off a feeling of "wrongness."

NATURAL TOOLS: Stingers; claws; venom

VOLTIX

HISTORY: Before becoming a bigtime criminal, Voltix specialized in small thefts, using his electrical powers to create illusions and distract those he wanted to rob.

PERSONALITY: Voltix is able to "feed" off virtually any type of energy, as opposed to needing a power Core, leaving him potentially immortal—as long as he can find power sources to feed off.

EQUIPMENT: Volt blaster; lightning

"QUIET, HE'S COMING. I'LL FRY HIM, AND YOU DO . . . WHATEVER IT IS YOU DO."

BREAKOUT

It seemed like just another day at Hero Factory. Furno and Rocka had brought in another criminal, Voltix, and locked him in jail. What they didn't know was that they were doing just what Voltix and his boss, Black Phantom, wanted. Once inside Hero Factory, Voltix managed to get his hands on Von Nebula's Black Hole Orb Staff. Using it, he blew a hole in the wall of the prison and all of the prisoners escaped.

Despite the best efforts of the Hero Factory personnel on hand, the flood of prisoners fleeing the facility could not be stopped. The best Stormer and the other Heroes could do was to hunt them down and bring them back. Equipped with special power-draining Hero cuffs, the team split up to chase the worst villains in the galaxy.

Bulk vs. Core Hunter; Furno vs. Jawblade; Breez vs. Thornraxx . . . the list of battles was a long one. When they were done, the most dangerous of the criminals had been defeated and returned to temporary prison quarters on Asteroid J-54. But the crisis was not yet over. . . .

Unknown to anyone but Zib, Rocka had stayed behind when the others left. His true identity, it turned out, was as a member of the secret Hero Recon Team. His mission had been to protect the Orb Staff. Now he suspected that the entire breakout was a distraction from something much bigger. And he was right.

Black Phantom had taken advantage of the confusion to infiltrate Hero Factory's inner workings. Rocka and the other Heroes eventually had to battle their way through the villain's Arachnix drones to try to stop him. In the end, with help from Evo, Rocka overpowered Black Phantom, but not before the cunning robot had transmitted the building plans for Hero Factory to an outside party. As yet, the identity of that robot or robots has not been discovered.

No one is under any illusions what this means. The complete details of Hero Factory's structure, defenses and every other confidential detail about its workings are now in enemy hands. The potential danger to the facility and everyone associated with it is overwhelming.

THE HISTOTRON SECRET FILES

GADGETS

HERO CUFFS: Unique devices developed in the Hero Factory labs, Hero cuffs drain the power of whomever they are attached to, making it easy to transport the villain to jail. They adjust automatically to fit any size wrists, and a built-in propulsion unit lets them actually pursue a target. Each Hero was issued a pair following the breakout. The only flaw with these devices is that they do not function underwater.

ARACHNIX DRONES: Small, four-legged robots created by Black Phantom. They are equipped with a front-mounted projectile launcher and are capable of replicating themselves. The Heroes battled a horde of these drones within Hero Factory while trying to apprehend Black Phantom.

PLACES

ASTEROID J-54: Prison asteroid used by Hero Factory to hold prisoners while the containment facilities in Makuhero City were being repaired following the breakout.

HIVE WORLD: Planet from which Thornaxx originated, and to which he returned after the breakout.

KOLLIX IV: Ice world to which Speeda Demon fled upon escaping from prison.

SIGMA SIGMA: Star system that was the location of Hero Factory's communications satellite, which was targeted by Splitface.

TANSARI VI: A planet known for its naturally occurring energy cells, it was Voltix's destination after his escape from Hero Factory.

BRAIN ATTACK

FURNO XL

HISTORY: Older and wiser, Furno has now become a trusted lieutenant to Stormer. In the wake of the evil brain invasion, Furno must take on more responsibility than ever before, as the menace is just too big and too widespread for one commander to handle it.

Furno is heavily involved in some of the early encounters with the brains, and fights valiantly in the defense of Hero Factory when the battle moves to Makuhero City.

EQUIPMENT: Flaming fire sword; fire shield; armored visor; spiked shoulder armor; Hero-Core locking clamps

ROCKA

HISTORY: Rocka has to pull double-duty in the face of the attack of the evil brains, as a warrior and as a tech wizard. His battles against the brains will go on to become Hero Factory legends, but his greatest contribution to the fight may be the Hero Recon Bikes with which he equips his comrades. These help the Heroes gain the advantage of surprise over the evil brains.

EQUIPMENT: 360-degree spinning razor shield; plasma blade sword; armored visor; Hero-Core locking clamps

BULK

HISTORY: The veteran of so many battles meets his greatest test, as the attack of the evil brains forces him to fight friends who have been taken over by the brains. Bulk has to put aside his feelings of loyalty and concentrate on his duty to Hero Factory and the galaxy. His raw power is desperately needed in this fight, as the brains attempt to use stealth and force of numbers to overcome the Heroes.

EQUIPMENT: Rotating laser drill; high-impact shield; armored visor; Hero-Core locking clamps

HISTORY: Like Furno, Breez had the misfortune to encounter the evil brains early in their invasion. She showed even greater bravery and resourcefulness than ever before and, also like Furno, gained greater respect from Stormer. Her days of working primarily at Hero Factory are over, as she is now considered a top field agent.

EQUIPMENT: Spinning razor saw; bow staff; armored visor; Hero-Core locking clamps

STORMER

HISTORY: The Alpha Team leader finds the evil brain attack strikes too close to home, as friends and worlds fall before the invaders. He is forced to take risks and make sacrifices he never would have contemplated before. But in the process, he learns to trust his team even more, including those Heroes he may have paid little attention to before. If Hero Factory survives this latest threat, it will be with a stronger Alpha Team leader and a stronger team of Heroes.

EQUIPMENT: Nano alloy sword with ice fangs; ice missile launcher; armored visor; Hero-Core locking clamps

HERO
SURGE

HISTORY: Surge has to put his doubts and questions aside as Hero Factory faces one of its greatest crises. His days as a rookie are left behind when Stormer needs every Hero to step up. But will he succeed? The thought of battling other Heroes, now turned evil by the brains, threatens to unleash the villain Surge has always feared lurks inside him.

EQUIPMENT: Dual plasma shooters; rotating lightning blades; jetpack wings; armored visor; Hero-Core locking clamps

HERO
EVO

HISTORY: Evo is determined to show his worth to the team as they battle the evil brains. Armed with new weapons technology, he will follow Furno's lead and be more aggressive in the fight. But Evo has to be careful: His new weapons are so powerful that he may cause more destruction than he prevents.

EQUIPMENT: White-hot vortex staff; armored underwater breathing visor; spiked armor; Hero-Core locking clamps

JET ROCKA

HISTORY: When the battle with the evil brains grows even more intense, Rocka is given new equipment by Zib to take the battle into the air. He may well be Hero Factory's last hope against the powerful Dragon Bolt the brains intend to use to conquer the Heroes. Rocka has to learn the technology quickly if he hopes to defeat a creature that has been flying all of its life.

EQUIPMENT: Jetpack; four missiles; dual plasma shooters; ion engines; super-sharp plasma wingblades

EVIL BRAINS

"YOU CANNOT COMPREHEND US, YOU CANNOT STOP US, WE HAVE ALREADY WON."

SUMMARY: Little is known about the origin of the evil brains, although it does seem that they were created artificially. We have learned that their intent is to eliminate Hero Factory so that their masters can use the facility to manufacture villains. The brains have proven skilled at creating chaos and are classified as a major threat.

ABILITIES: The brains are able to take over the minds of other beings by latching onto their heads. Their prehensile tails pack a punch as well, and their skins are poisonous. The only way to dislodge a brain from its host is to strike it on the second red spike on its back.

PYROX

HISTORY: This bull-like creature was a menace long before it ever encountered a brain. But once the brain attached itself to its skull, Pyrox became a fiery, destructive force to be reckoned with. Its sheer raw power makes it more than a match even for a team of Heroes. Add to that its flaming might and it is like nothing ever seen before.

PERSONALITY: Pyrox is a like a runaway spacecraft—all one can hope to do is stay out of its way.

NATURAL TOOLS: Horns; rotating flame staff; fire claws; lava shoulder armor

SCAROX

HISTORY: Scarox was a simple dune crawler until an evil brain transformed it into a venomous spider beast. Now it is a one-creature engine of devastation, a threat even Hero Factory may not be able to stop. Despite Zib's best efforts at refining and upgrading Hero armor, he has yet to find an alloy that can stand up to Scarox's fangs. Already, multiple Heroes have fallen before the power of this insectoid. How many more will follow them before Alpha Team finds a way to defeat it?

PERSONALITY: Sneaky by nature used to striking at prey from beneath the cover of a sand dune, Scarox still prefers to attack from ambush.

NATURAL TOOLS: Armor-piercing fang; poisonous venom; spiked legs; striking blades

VILLAIN
OGRUM

HISTORY: Experts are still divided on what Ogrum was before the evil brains found it, but there is no doubt what it is now: a bizarre plant-animal hybrid, able to use the most dangerous weapons of both flora and fauna against the Heroes. Its ability to blend in with jungle foliage makes it particularly dangerous, and it has mastered the art of the surprise attack.

NATURAL TOOLS: Vines; claw feet; wrecking mace

VILLAIN
BRUIZER

HISTORY: This colossus of stone has been transformed by the evil brains into a raging rock monster. Bruizer is probably the easiest of the brains' victims to find, as it leaves a path of destruction that can be seen from space wherever it goes. Apparently, Bruizers' species does not require sleep, food, or water to survive. It lives to destroy, and the brains have given it an unlimited opportunity to do so.

NATURAL TOOLS: Rock-smasher fist; rock shoulder armor; razor-spikes

AQUAGON

HISTORY: Originally a harmless sea creature, the evil brains have made Aquagon anything but. It is a vicious sea beast, designed to strike from the water. Its sole weakness is its inability to breathe air and rapid dehydration when on land. But compared to its sheer strength and ability to drag a Hero to the bottom of the ocean almost at will, the knowledge provides little comfort.

NATURAL TOOLS: Spiked shoulder armor; stinging tentacles

EQUIPMENT: Dual sword staff

FROST BEAST

HISTORY: On its home planet, the creature now codenamed "Frost Beast" was the dominant predator. Transformed by the evil brains, it is now an icy threat whose heart is as cold as a blizzard. Its very touch is so cold that it can freeze and crack metal, and its assortment of natural weaponry makes it one of the brains' most dangerous pawns.

NATURAL TOOLS: Spiked ice teeth; claws

EQUIPMENT: Frost blade; ice armor

DRAGON BOLT

HISTORY: This dragon-like creature has been transformed by the evil brains into a true flying serpent of legend. Armed with razor-sharp tail spikes and mighty storm wings, Dragon Bolt is the brains' secret weapon against the Heroes. Fierce and almost immune to pain, it might spell doom for the grounded Heroes unless Jet Rocka can find some way to defeat it. Little is known about the beast or its origins, but one can be sure Zib will be researching it if Hero Factory survives the encounter.

NATURAL TOOLS: Teeth; tail spikes; wings

BRAIN ATTACK

From an unknown corner of the galaxy comes a swarm of evil brains. Their power: taking over the mind of any robot, beast, or creature to which they attach themselves, transforming the innocent being into a force of evil.

Their target: Hero Factory.

They strike without warning, turning whole populations into menaces. No world or environment is safe, as both intelligent robots and near-mindless beasts become victims of the evil brains.

Stormer assembles a team of Heroes and leads them into battle with the brains. But the attackers are too many and too powerful, and the Heroes are forced to retreat to Hero Factory. There, with the aid of Hero Recon Bikes designed by Rocka, they manage to make a stand.

At first, it seems like they are about to save the day. The Heroes succeed in driving the brain-controlled robots to the rooftop of Hero Factory. But once there, they face their greatest challenge yet: the coming of Dragon Bolt!

OBJECT

HERO-CORE LOCKING CLAMPS

Following their battles with Core Hunter, the Heroes of Alpha Team realize their Hero Cores were vulnerable to theft or destruction by well-equipped villains. With the aid of Zib, Rocka designed these special clamps that use electro-magnetism to hold the Cores in place. Heroes can now go into battle relatively certain their Hero Cores will be safe.

The Hero Factory chapter book series has introduced new characters, new locations, and new dangers into the universe of Stormer and his team. Here is a rundown of some of the robots and places the Heroes have encountered in these tales:

SECRET MISSION #1: THE DOOM BOX
SECRET MISSION #2: LEGION OF DARKNESS
SECRET MISSION #3: COLLISION COURSE
SECRET MISSION #4: ROBOT RAMPAGE
SECRET MISSION #5: MIRROR WORLD

LOCATIONS

CITADEL: Von Nebula's headquarters on Dark Mirror World.

MIRROR WORLD: Unofficial designation for a parallel dimension in which Hero Factory was defeated in its early years by the Legion of Darkness and Von Nebula now dominate a large portion of the galaxy.

GRONND: Planet where the *Valiant* was designed and constructed.

TRANQUIS VII: Planet invaded by the evil brains. Tranquis VII had been a thriving planet before an environmental disaster wiped out most of the wildlife. The robot residents stayed and rebuilt their world.

TRANQUIS: Capital city of Tranquis VII. It is largely destroyed by rampaging robots imperfectly controlled by evil brains.

VALIANT: Cruiser designed to protect the frontier worlds in the event Hero Factory was not available to do so. It is armed with mass drivers and high-intensity lasers, and powered by a tri-nuclear fusion engine. Its crew is taken over by evil brains and it is set on a collision course with Hero Factory.

CHARACTERS

AQUAX: Captain of the *Valiant* and an old friend of Stormer's. He is unaware that the construction of his ship was all part of a larger conspiracy against Hero Factory.

ARCTUR: Leader of the organization that created the Doom Box. It is Arctur's decision to split the box into pieces and conceal it, once he realizes its devastating potential. Later, he manipulates Core Hunter into attempting to reassemble it.

DENEB: A member of the secret organization which created the Doom Box. Deneb objects to the dismantling of the box and secretly records the locations in which the parts of it would be hidden.

DUMACC: Scientist employed at a hidden base in Tranquis on a secret weapons project.

GEB: Manager of a refueling station on a desert world frequently used as a hideout by Core Hunter.

KARTER: Assistant to Dumacc and later exposed as part of an interplanetary conspiracy. He is arrested and sent to Hero Factory, where he sabotages equipment and sends part of Alpha Team into a parallel dimension.

KIRCH: Security chief of the *Valiant* and the first member of the crew to be taken over by an evil brain.

XERA: Science officer of the *Valiant*, whose curiosity leads to the evil brains making it onboard the vessel.

The records of Hero Factory contain accounts of many great Hero vs. villain battles. But many fights still remain in the category of "WHAT IF?" Heroes vs. Heroes; villains vs. villains . . . battles that have *never* been fought, but could happen one day . . .

In this chapter, we will look at eleven matchups, including stats for each fighter and special moves. Who do *you* think would win?

FACE OFF!

STORMER 1.0 VS. FURNO 1.0

Although they are now good teammates, Stormer and Furno often argued when the rookie first joined the team. Heroes don't fight other Heroes, but WHAT IF these two had battled? Who do you think would win?

PRESTON STORMER

HOME: Makuhero City

AFFILIATION: Hero Factory, Alpha Team Leader

SPECIES: Robot

WEAPONS: Multifunctional ice weapon

SPECIAL MOVE: Stormer Strike, a paralyzing blow

STRENGTH	▮▮▮▮▮▮▮▮ ▯▯▯
AGILITY	▮▮▮▮▮▮▮▮ ▯▯▯
INTELLIGENCE	▮▮▮▮▮▮▮▮▮ ▯▯
CONTROL	▮▮▮▮▮▮▮▮▮ ▯▯
COURAGE	▮▮▮▮▮▮▮▮▮▮ ▯
TOUGHNESS	▮▮▮▮▮▮▮▮ ▯▯▯

WILLIAM FURNO

HOME: Makuhero City

AFFILIATION: Hero Factory, Alpha Team

SPECIES: Robot

WEAPONS: Dual fire shooter

SPECIAL MOVE: Furno Flip

STRENGTH	▮▮▮
AGILITY	▮▮▮
INTELLIGENCE	▮▮▮▮
CONTROL	▮▮▮▮
COURAGE	▮
TOUGHNESS	▮▮

FIRE LORD VS. WITCH DOCTOR

These two villains never met until they were in prison together. Both wanted vengeance on Hero Factory and could have seen the other as an obstacle to be eliminated. Here's how their fight might have shaped up:

FIRE LORD

HOME: Tallos 5

AFFILIATION: None

SPECIES: Mining robot

WEAPONS: Lava sphere shooter; lava flamethrower

SPECIAL MOVE: Fist of Flame

STRENGTH	▮▮▮▮▮▮▮▮❚❚
AGILITY	▮▮▮▮▮▮▮❚❚❚
INTELLIGENCE	▮▮▮▮▮❚❚❚❚❚
CONTROL	▮▮▮▮▮❚❚❚❚❚
COURAGE	▮▮▮▮▮▮▮▮▮❚
TOUGHNESS	▮▮▮▮▮▮▮▮❚❚

WITCH DOCTOR

HOME: Makuhero City

AFFILIATION: None

SPECIES: Robot

WEAPONS: Skull staff

SPECIAL MOVE: Skull Double Thrust

STRENGTH	
AGILITY	
INTELLIGENCE	
CONTROL	
COURAGE	
TOUGHNESS	

STRINGER VS. BLACK PHANTOM

Rocka ended up being the Hero who challenged Black Phantom inside Hero Factory. But WHAT IF Stringer had made it back in time and been the one to battle the villain instead?

JIMI STRINGER

HOME: Makuhero City

AFFILIATION: Hero Factory, Alpha Team

SPECIES: Robot

WEAPONS: Sonic blaster

SPECIAL MOVE: Sonic Boom

STRENGTH	▮▮▮
AGILITY	▮▮
INTELLIGENCE	▮▮
CONTROL	▮▮
COURAGE	▮▮
TOUGHNESS	▮▮▮

BLACK PHANTOM

HOME: Unknown

AFFILIATION: Legion of Darkness

SPECIES: Robot

WEAPONS: Razor Sabre Mace Staff; sabre strikers

SPECIAL MOVE: Dual Sabre Slash

STRENGTH	░░░░░░░░▓▓
AGILITY	░░░░░░░▓▓▓
INTELLIGENCE	░░░░░░░░▓▓
CONTROL	░░░░░░▓▓▓▓
COURAGE	░░░░░░▓▓▓▓
TOUGHNESS	░░░░░░░░▓▓

FURNO XL VS. FROST BEAST

Furno is more powerful than ever before in his XL armor—but in the Frost Beast, he faces a completely savage creature from the icy wastes. Can Hero Factory training prevail against the wild rage of the Frost Beast?

FURNO XL

HOME: Makuhero City

AFFILIATION: Hero Factory, Alpha Team

SPECIES: Robot

WEAPONS: Flaming fire sword; fire shield

SPECIAL MOVE: Inferno Blast

STRENGTH	⬛⬛⬛⬛⬛⬛⬛⬜⬜
AGILITY	⬛⬛⬛⬛⬛⬛⬛⬜⬜
INTELLIGENCE	⬛⬛⬛⬛⬛⬛⬜⬜⬜
CONTROL	⬛⬛⬛⬛⬛⬛⬜⬜⬜
COURAGE	⬛⬛⬛⬛⬛⬛⬛⬛⬜
TOUGHNESS	⬛⬛⬛⬛⬛⬛⬛⬛⬜

FROST BEAST

HOME: Unknown

AFFILIATION: Evil brains

SPECIES: Robot

WEAPONS: Frost blade

SPECIAL MOVE: Icy Grip of Doom

STRENGTH	■■■■■■■■□
AGILITY	■■■■■□□□
INTELLIGENCE	■■■■□□□□
CONTROL	■■■□□□□□
COURAGE	■■■■■■■■□
TOUGHNESS	■■■■■■■■■

BULK VS. SURGE

Surge has often worried he might turn into a villain one day. If he did, Bulk might be sent out to match his raw power against Surge's electrical energy. Let's hope this never happens. But just in case, let's take a look. . . .

DUNKAN BULK

HOME: Makuhero City

AFFILIATION: Hero Factory, Alpha Team

SPECIES: Robot

WEAPONS: Metal sphere shooter

SPECIAL MOVE: Bulk Reverse Slam

STRENGTH	||||||||▮▮
AGILITY	||||||▮▮▮▮
INTELLIGENCE	|||||||▮▮▮
CONTROL	|||||||▮▮▮
COURAGE	|||||||||▮
TOUGHNESS	||||||||▮▮

MARK SURGE

HOME: Makuhero City

AFFILIATION: Hero Factory, Alpha Team

SPECIES: Robot

WEAPONS: Electrical shield; lightning weapon

SPECIAL MOVE: High-Voltage Strike

STRENGTH

AGILITY

INTELLIGENCE

CONTROL

COURAGE

TOUGHNESS

PYROX VS. BRUIZER

Which is tougher: the bludgeoning power of rock or the searing fury of flame? Only the outcome of this "WHAT-IF" fight can reveal the answer, as two of the evil brains' pawns go head to head! Who do you think will win?

PYROX

HOME: Unknown	
AFFILIATION: Evil brains	
SPECIES: Robot	
WEAPONS: Rotating flame staff	
SPECIAL MOVE: Ultra-fast Power Charge	

STRENGTH ▮▮▮▮▮▮▮▮▮▮
AGILITY ▮▮▮▮▮▮▮▮▮▮
INTELLIGENCE ▮▮▮▮▮▮▮▮▮▮
CONTROL ▮▮▮▮▮▮▮▮▮▮
COURAGE ▮▮▮▮▮▮▮▮▮▮
TOUGHNESS ▮▮▮▮▮▮▮▮▮▮

Bruizer

HOME: Unknown

AFFILIATION: Evil brains

SPECIES: Robot

WEAPONS: Razor-spikes

SPECIAL MOVE: Stone Smash

STRENGTH	
AGILITY	
INTELLIGENCE	
CONTROL	
COURAGE	
TOUGHNESS	

ROCKA VS. CORE HUNTER

Core Hunter is always a threat to escape from prison, and any Hero might be called upon to take him down. This fight is based on an actual simulation done in the Hero Factory virtual training rooms.

ROCKA

HOME: Makuhero City

AFFILIATION: Hero Factory, Alpha Team and Hero Recon Team

SPECIES: Robot

WEAPONS: Crossbow

SPECIAL MOVE: Midair Somersault Shot

STRENGTH	III
AGILITY	II
INTELLIGENCE	III
CONTROL	II
COURAGE	II
TOUGHNESS	III

CORE HUNTER

HOME: Unknown

AFFILIATION: None

SPECIES: Robot

WEAPONS: Core-remover tool

SPECIAL MOVE: Stealth Strike

STRENGTH ▌▌▌

AGILITY ▌▌

INTELLIGENCE ▌▌

CONTROL ▌▌

COURAGE ▌▌▌

TOUGHNESS ▌▌

VOLTIX VS. XT4

These two were teammates in the Legion of Darkness, but no one is ever really "friends" with XT4. If it came down to a fight between these two villains, who would be left standing?

VOLTIX

HOME: Unknown

AFFILIATION: Legion of Darkness

SPECIES: Robot

WEAPONS: Volt blaster; lightning whip

SPECIAL MOVE: Short-Circuit Slam

STRENGTH ▮▮▮

AGILITY ▮▮▮

INTELLIGENCE ▮▮▮▮

CONTROL ▮▮▮▮

COURAGE ▮▮▮▮

TOUGHNESS ▮▮

XT4

HOME: Makuro IV

AFFILIATION: Legion of Darkness

SPECIES: Industrial robot

WEAPONS: Two striking blades; laser slicer; razor disc slicer

SPECIAL MOVE: Whirling Quad-Strike

STRENGTH	████████ ▌▌
AGILITY	████████ ▌▌
INTELLIGENCE	███████ ▌▌▌
CONTROL	████████ ▌▌
COURAGE	████████ ▌▌
TOUGHNESS	███████ ▌▌▌

BREEZ VS. MELTDOWN

Breez fought Meltdown briefly in New Stellac City, but they have never faced each other one-on-one. If they met again on the battlefield, who would win—and who would fall?

NATALIE BREEZ

HOME: Makuhero City

AFFILIATION: Hero Factory, Alpha Team

SPECIES: Robot

WEAPONS: Energized dual boomerang

SPECIAL MOVE: Sidewinder Sweeping Kick

STRENGTH	▌▌▌▌
AGILITY	▌▌
INTELLIGENCE	▌▌▌
CONTROL	▌▌
COURAGE	▌▌
TOUGHNESS	▌▌▌

MELTDOWN

HOME: Unnamed frontier world

AFFILIATION: Von Nebula's gang

SPECIES: Robot

WEAPONS: Radioactive sludge shooter; meteor blaster

SPECIAL MOVE: Hard Radiation Hammer

STRENGTH ▮▮▮

AGILITY ▮▮▮

INTELLIGENCE ▮▮▮▮

CONTROL ▮▮▮▮▮▮

COURAGE ▮▮▮▮▮

TOUGHNESS ▮▮

EVO VS. OGRUM

Evo is always looking for new challenges, and he has one this time as he faces the plant-animal hybrid that is Ogrum. Can Evo overcome the evil brilliance of the brain and find Ogrum's weakness in time?

Evo

HOME: Makuhero City

AFFILIATION: Hero Factory, Alpha Team

SPECIES: Robot

WEAPONS: White-hot vortex staff

SPECIAL MOVE: Cyclone Slam

STRENGTH	
AGILITY	
INTELLIGENCE	
CONTROL	
COURAGE	
TOUGHNESS	

OGRUM

HOME: Unknown

AFFILIATION: Evil brains

SPECIES: Robot

WEAPONS: Wrecking mace

SPECIAL MOVE: Vine-Whip Toss

STRENGTH	‖‖‖‖‖‖‖‖‖■■
AGILITY	‖‖‖‖‖‖‖‖‖■
INTELLIGENCE	‖‖‖‖■■■■■
CONTROL	‖‖‖‖■■■■■
COURAGE	‖‖‖‖‖‖‖‖‖■
TOUGHNESS	‖‖‖‖‖‖‖‖■■

STORMER XL VS. VON NEBULA

In his new XL armor, Stormer is more powerful than before. But could he defeat Von Nebula on his own, or would the master of the black hole win in the end?

PRESTON STORMER XL

HOME: Makuhero City

AFFILIATION: Hero Factory, Alpha Team Leader

SPECIES: Robot

WEAPONS: Power sword; plasma gun

SPECIAL MOVE: XL Extreme Chop

STRENGTH	■■
AGILITY	■■■
INTELLIGENCE	■■
CONTROL	■■
COURAGE	■
TOUGHNESS	■

VON NEBULA

HOME: Makuhero City

AFFILIATION: None

SPECIES: Robot

WEAPONS: Black Hole Orb Staff

SPECIAL MOVE: Gravity Crusher

STRENGTH	
AGILITY	
INTELLIGENCE	
CONTROL	
COURAGE	
TOUGHNESS	

End Transmission ...